Disappearing Doll!

"Did anyone see what happened to Hollywood Heather?" Deirdre cried out.

"It's just a doll," Trina said.

"Just a doll?" Deirdre gasped. "Is the Statue of Liberty just a statue? Is the Great Wall of China just a wall? Is Johnny Appleseed just an apple?"

"He's not an apple," Andrea said slowly. "I think he planted apple trees or something."

"Whatever!" Deirdre cried.

The girls looked for Hollywood Heather for half an hour. But she was nowhere to be found.

"If anyone in this room took Hollywood Heather," Deirdre said, "tell me now."

Join the CLUE CREW
& solve these other cases!

Nancy Drew AND THE CLUE CREW

#1

Sleepover Sleuths

BY CAROLYN KEENE

ILLUSTRATED BY MACKY PAMINTUAN

Aladdin Paperbacks
New York London Toronto Sydney

❦ ALADDIN PAPERBACKS

An imprint of Simon & Schuster Children's Publishing Division

1230 Avenue of the Americas, New York, NY 10020

Text copyright © 2006 by Simon & Schuster, Inc.

Illustrations copyright © 2006 by Macky Pamintuan

All rights reserved, including the right of reproduction in whole or in part in any form.

ALADDIN PAPERBACKS, NANCY DREW AND THE CLUE CREW,

and colophon are trademarks of Simon & Schuster, Inc.

NANCY DREW is a registered trademark of Simon & Schuster, Inc.

Designed by Lisa Vega

The text of this book was set in ITC Stone Informal.

Manufactured in the United States of America

First Aladdin Paperbacks edition June 2006

10 9 8 7 6 5 4

Library of Congress Control Number 2005931092

ISBN-13: 978-1-4169-1255-2

ISBN-10: 1-4169-1255-X

CONTENTS

Sleepover Sleuths

CHAPTER ONE

"Guess What?"

"Wow, Nancy," George Fayne said as she raced down the school steps. "I don't know how you do it."

"Do what?" eight-year-old Nancy Drew asked.

"As if you didn't know!" Bess Marvin giggled. She tossed her blond hair as she held her books in both arms. "You guessed the lunch in the school cafeteria again!"

"Oh, that!" Nancy said with a smile.

It was Friday afternoon and Nancy, Bess, and George were leaving River Heights Elementary School. Bess and George were Nancy's two best friends. They were also cousins. The three girls were all in the same third grade class.

They had been friends since kindergarten.

"It was easy to guess," Nancy explained. "The halls smelled fishy today, so that meant we were having fish sticks. And Mrs. Nicholson the lunch lady makes potato salad every three weeks."

"What are we having on Monday?" George quizzed.

"Macaroni and cheese," Nancy replied. "I saw the boxes behind the counter today."

"Yummy!" Bess said. "But I don't want to think about Monday yet."

She glanced at her favorite blue watch. It told the time all over the world. Bess loved all sorts of gadgets. She also loved to build her own.

"It's exactly one minute after three o'clock in the United States," Bess reported. "Which means the weekend has just begun!"

Nancy brushed some reddish-blond hair out of her eyes. "What are you guys doing this weekend?" she asked.

"I'm building a butterfly mobile to hang over my bed," Bess said, her blue eyes flashing.

"There's a neat new game I want to check

out on the computer," George said. "It's called 'Space Cadets from Planet Weirdo'!"

"My cousin, the computer geek!" Bess joked.

"And proud of it!" George declared. "What are you doing this weekend, Nancy?"

"Maybe I'll give Chocolate Chip a bath," Nancy said. "That naughty puppy rolled around in something stinky yesterday—"

"Nancy, Bess, George!" a voice interrupted her.

Nancy and her friends spun around. Deirdre Shannon and her best friend Madison Foley were running across the schoolyard toward them.

Deirdre was in Mrs. Ramirez's class with Nancy, Bess, and George. She was nice, even though Nancy thought she was a bit spoiled. Her mom and dad gave her lots of things. She even had her own Web site, called Dishing with Deirdre. Deirdre wrote about everything on her Web site—from her dance recitals to her dentist appointments!

"Hi, Deirdre," Nancy said. "What's up?"

Deirdre and Madison stopped when they reached the girls. Deirdre tilted her head a little and asked, "Do any of you have a City Girls doll?"

Nancy, Bess, and George traded smiles.

The City Girls were the most awesome dolls ever! Each one came with cool clothes and accessories. And they were each named after a city in the United States.

"I have Chicago Cheryl," Nancy said. "The doll with the purple coat and matching hat. Purple is my favorite color."

Madison nodded at Nancy's purple jacket and sneakers. "As if we didn't know!" she said with a grin.

"I have Oklahoma City Olivia," George added. "She wears the neatest denim outfit and cowboy boots!"

"Honolulu Haley is my City Girl," Bess piped in. "She came with her own little flip-flops and surfboard."

Deirdre rolled her eyes. "I know, I know," she said. "I know all the City Girls. I have five of them myself!"

"Then why did you ask us, *Dee-Dee?*" George asked.

Nancy jabbed George with her elbow. She knew Deirdre hated the nickname Dee-Dee.

"It's *Deirdre!*" Deirdre said.

"How would you like it if we called you *Georgia?*" Madison asked George.

George scrunched her nose when she heard her real name. "No, thanks," she said. "I'll stick with George."

Deirdre reached into her backpack. She pulled out three white envelopes. "Tomorrow night, eight o'clock," she said. "Bring your sleeping bag, toothbrush, and City Girls doll!"

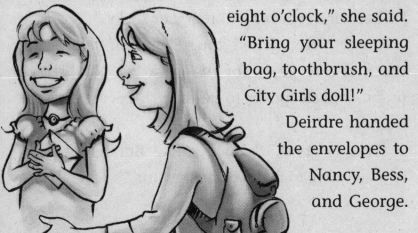

Deirdre handed the envelopes to Nancy, Bess, and George.

Then she and Madison ran across the yard to Kendra Jackson.

"What are these, Nancy?" Bess asked.

"I can't guess everything," Nancy said, smiling. "So there's only one way to find out."

Nancy tore open her envelope and pulled out a card. Her eyes widened as she read the pink writing. It was an invitation to a birthday sleepover on Saturday night!

Bess and George pulled out their own invitations and shrieked.

"Are we lucky or what?" Bess cried. "We have never been invited to any of Deirdre's parties before!"

"Deirdre may be spoiled," George said. "But I'll bet her sleepover will rock our socks!"

Nancy was excited too. Five minutes ago she had zero plans for the weekend. Now she had a cool sleepover to go to with her two best friends!

"This is great," Nancy said. "But I wonder why we have to bring our City Girls."

❀ ❀ ❀

"Toothbrush?" Hannah asked.

"Check!" Nancy answered.

"Flannel pj's with cupcake design?" Hannah asked.

Nancy peeked inside her big purple backpack and smiled. "Check!" she said.

It was seven fifteen on Saturday night. Hannah Gruen was standing in Nancy's lavender and white bedroom, making sure she had everything she needed for the sleepover.

Hannah had been the Drews' housekeeper ever since Nancy's mother died, when she was three years old. Hannah took such good care of her that she was almost like a mother to Nancy.

"Sleeping bag?" Hannah quizzed.

"Sleep?" Nancy cried. "We're not going to sleep, Hannah!"

Hannah raised an eyebrow. "Sleeping bag?" she asked again.

"Check," Nancy said as she tossed her rolled-up sleeping bag on her bed.

"Now, are you sure you have everything?" Hannah asked.

"Sure, I'm sure," Nancy said. She glanced at the clock on her bedside table. "But I'd better go now. Daddy is probably waiting in the car."

Nancy shrugged her backpack over her hoodie. She tucked her sleeping bag under her arm and bounded down the stairs. "I am so totally psyched, Hannah!" she called. "This is going to be the best City Girls party in the—"

Nancy froze on the stairs.

"Oops," she said. "I almost forgot my City Girls doll!"

Hannah stood at the top of the stairs. She pulled Chicago Cheryl from behind her back. "I was wondering how long it would take you to notice!" she said with a laugh.

Nancy tucked Chicago Cheryl under her free arm. She darted out the door and into her dad's car. After they buckled their seatbelts, Mr. Drew drove to the Marvin house to pick up Bess and George. Soon all three girls were sitting in the backseat with their sleepover gear and dolls.

George was wearing all denim, just like Oklahoma City Olivia. Bess wore a little red silk flower in her hair like Honolulu Haley.

"Why does everyone have to bring a City Girls doll to the party?" Mr. Drew asked as he drove.

Mr. Drew was a busy lawyer. But he was never too busy to spend time with Nancy.

"City Girls rule, Daddy!" Nancy said. "Each one is different."

"Anchorage Abby is from Alaska, so she comes with furry boots," Bess said. "And Malibu Marcy has real sand between her toes!"

"That's gross," George said.

"But the most awesome City Girls doll," Nancy said, "is Hollywood Heather!"

"Oooh!" cried Bess.

"Ahhh!" exclaimed George.

There were only a few Hollywood Heathers made in the whole United States. She was very special and very expensive.

"I heard Heather's poncho is made out of real cashmere," Bess said. "That's wool from goats."

"I heard she has real leather boots!" George said.

"And sterling silver earrings!" Nancy put in.

"I read on the City Girls Web site that there's only one Hollywood Heather left in the whole country," George added.

Mr. Drew slowed down as he drove up a tree-lined street. He stopped the car in front of a huge white house.

"This is the Shannon house, girls," Mr. Drew said.

Nancy leaned over Bess and George to look out the window. "Wow!" she exclaimed.

A red carpet lined the path leading to the house. There were huge lights on the

lawn and cardboard cutouts of famous movie stars!

Deirdre stepped out of the house wearing dark sunglasses and a fancy feather boa. As Nancy, Bess, and George walked up the red carpet, Mr. Shannon snapped pictures of them. Nancy guessed they were for Deirdre's Web site. Mr. Shannon was a lawyer, just like Nancy's dad.

"Nancy, George, Bess!" Deirdre called, swinging her boa. "Are you ready for your close-up? I mean—sleepover?"

"What's up with this?" Bess whispered to Nancy and George.

"I think Deirdre has gone Hollywood," George whispered.

The flash from Mr. Shannon's camera made Nancy see spots. "I don't get it," she said as she blinked. "Isn't this supposed to be a City Girls party?"

CHAPTER TWO

Sleepover Secret

"Hi, girls!" Mrs. Shannon said as they entered the house. Deirdre's mom was wearing a pink sweater and black stretch pants. Her brown hair was combed in a neat flip.

"Hello," Nancy said in her most polite voice.

"Why don't you bring your gear down to the basement?" Mrs. Shannon said. "That's where the fun is!"

"And the snacks!" Deirdre added.

Deirdre waved them to the door leading to the basement. George pointed to a dark blue duffel bag against the wall. "Looks like someone forgot their bag," she said.

Deirdre squeezed her nose and said, "That's Trina Vanderhoof's smelly basketball bag. I'm making her keep it upstairs so it doesn't stink up the sleepover."

Nancy felt something tickle her ankle. She looked down and saw a furry white cat. It purred softly as it rubbed against Nancy's leg.

"She looks like a marshmallow!" Nancy cooed.

"You guessed her name," Deirdre said. "It's Marshmallow!"

"Can Marshmallow come to the party?" George asked.

"I wish," Deirdre sighed. "Trina is allergic to cats."

Trina Vanderhoof was in Mrs. Bailey's third grade class at school. She was so tall that she played basketball with the fourth grade boys at recess. She was also becoming very good friends with Deirdre.

The girls walked down the narrow staircase to the basement. The room was decorated with silver and gold balloons and big cardboard stars. A sign on the wall read, HOORAY FOR HOLLYWOOD! There was also a big-screen TV, a DVD player, a sofa against one wall, and shelves filled with books and games. A table was piled high with presents for Deirdre.

Nancy saw more girls sitting on the floor with their dolls. She recognized Trina, Kendra Jackson, Madison Foley, Andrea Wu, and Marcy Rubin. Nancy knew everyone from school—except a little girl running around in footsie pajamas.

"Marcy pours orange juice on her cornflakes!" the little girl sang out loud. "Marcy is afraid of spiders!"

"That's my little sister, Cassidy," Marcy groaned. "My parents went to a concert tonight, so I had to bring her."

Cassidy began jumping up and down. "Marcy sleeps with a teddy bear! Marcy bites her toenails—"

"Put a sock in it!" Marcy cut in.

One more girl with copper red hair and freckles

entered the room. It was Nadine Nardo. Everyone knew Nadine wanted to be an actress when she grew up, so her nickname was "Nadine the Drama Queen."

"I love those stars!" Nadine said, pointing to the wall. "They remind me of . . . *me*!"

Nancy, Bess, and George dropped their gear on the floor. They pulled out their birthday presents for Deirdre and placed them on the table with the other gifts. Nearby, on a smaller table, stood something covered with a long white cloth.

"What's under this?" Nancy asked. She was about to lift the cloth when—

"Don't peek! It's a surprise!" Deirdre shouted. She turned to Cassidy, who was creeping toward the table. "Anyone who peeks underneath will grow warts on their nose and hair on their tongue!"

"Pizza time!" Mrs. Shannon sang as she breezed into the room. Behind her Mr. Shannon carried three pizza boxes in his arms.

As the girls sat on the floor to eat their slices, Nancy kept glancing at the small table. "I wonder what's under that cloth," she whispered.

"I hope we find out soon," Bess whispered back.

The girls ate three kinds of pies: pepperoni, mushroom, and extra cheese. Cassidy pressed two pepperonis against her eyes and ran around the room shouting, "I'm an alien from planet Pizza Pie!"

"You mean space cadet," Marcy muttered.

Nancy took a sip of fruit punch. Then she asked, "Where's your City Girls doll, Deirdre?"

"I couldn't decide which one to bring down," Deirdre said with a shrug.

That's a strange excuse, Nancy thought as she picked up another slice.

The girls finished all three pizzas. Then Deirdre opened her presents. She loved the dotted stationery set that Nancy gave her. After all the presents were opened, everyone changed into their pj's and had a pajama fashion show.

"Here is Bess modeling her favorite pink pj's," Nadine announced with a French accent. "Merci, Bess!"

Bess twirled like a supermodel. Then George pretended to walk down a runway in her red and white striped pajamas. Following her was Nancy in her favorite cupcake pj's.

Of all the pajamas, Nadine's orange ones were the brightest. And Nancy thought her slippers with the unicorn heads were the most fun!

"Say cheese!" Deirdre said. She held up her camera. "I want a picture of everyone with their City Girls dolls!"

The girls crowded together. They smiled as they held up their dolls.

"Cheese . . . with pepperoni!" Trina joked.

Deirdre stared at Trina's doll. "What is *that*?" she asked.

"Indianapolis Ivy," Trina answered. "My City Girls doll."

"I know all the City Girls dolls," Deirdre said. "And I never heard of Indianapolis Ivy."

"I've never heard of Indianapolis Ivy, either," Madison said.

"Are you saying my doll is fake?" Trina asked.

Nancy hoped Deirdre and Trina wouldn't fight.

"You guys!" Nancy said. "What difference does it make, as long as we all love our dolls?"

Just then Trina threw back her head and let out a big sneeze. "Ah, ah, ah-choooo!"

"Meeeeow!"

Nancy turned around. She saw Marshmallow the cat padding around the room.

"You know I'm allergic to cats." Trina sniffed.

"My parents must have left the basement door open," Deirdre said. "Sorry, Marshmallow. It's all Trina's fault you can't come to the party." She picked up the cat and carried her up the basement stairs.

Madison giggled. But Trina muttered something like, "Whatever, Dee-Dee."

"Um . . . let's play another game!" Nancy blurted out.

The game they all played was called, "Find the Prize." The girls separated into teams. Then they set out to find a goody bag that Mrs. Shannon had hidden somewhere in the room.

Nancy, Bess, and George were on the same team.

"Where do we start looking?" George asked.

Nancy's eyes darted around the room. She saw something sparkling on the carpet and kneeled down for a closer look. It was a tiny clump of green glitter. A few inches away was another speck of glitter.

"I think I see a trail!" Nancy whispered. "Let's see where it leads."

The girls followed the glitter to a bookshelf. "Look! There's more glitter on one of the shelves," Nancy cried. Tucked between two books was the goody bag—decorated with green glitter!

"Found it!" Nancy called out.

Everyone watched as Nancy opened the goody bag. It was filled with three pink bangle bracelets and three sets of matching barrettes.

"Pretty!" Cassidy exclaimed.

"How did you find it so fast?" Kendra asked.

"Nancy followed the glitter trail!" George said.

"You're good at finding things, Nancy," Andrea said.

"And guessing things," Bess added.

"I guess I am!" Nancy said with a smile.

"You guys!" Deirdre cut in. She was wearing her feathery boa as she stood next to the mystery table. "It's time for my super-big surprise!"

"Yes!" Nancy cheered softly under her breath. They would finally find out what was underneath the cloth!

The girls sat in a semicircle by the table. Deirdre waved her boa and said, "Please welcome . . . the one and only . . . the one of a kind . . . and very expensive . . ."

She whipped off the white drape and shouted, "Hollywood Heather!"

Everyone gasped.

Nancy stared at the doll. Her blond hair hung in curls over her shoulders.

Her blue eyes were so bright they twinkled. She was wearing an apple green poncho, a white leather skirt, and matching white boots. Her silver hoop earrings glowed against her suntanned cheeks.

"It's her!" Nancy swooned.

"It's Hollywood Heather!" Bess sighed.

"That explains the Hollywood party!" Kendra said.

Just then a slipper hit the back wall. Nancy could see it was a unicorn slipper.

"It's not fair!" a voice shouted. "It's not fair!"

CHAPTER THREE

Hello, Dolly!

Nancy recognized the slipper and the voice. Nadine Nardo marched over with her hands planted on her hips. Her bottom lip jutted out in a pout.

"I was saving my allowance for Hollywood Heather!" Nadine said. "I'm going to be a star someday. So I should have Hollywood Heather!"

"Well," Deirdre said, "she's mine."

"Oh, great," George whispered. "This is the second fight so far."

"Why can't we all be friends?" Bess whispered.

"Don't you like your New York Nikki doll?" Nancy asked Nadine. "She has a cool leather jacket and jeans. And her brown hair is so long and shiny."

"Sure, I like her," Nadine said. "But I can have more than one City Girls doll."

"You can play with Hollywood Heather any time, Nadine." Deirdre sighed. She then yelled up the basement stairs, "Mom! Time for cake!"

While the girls admired Hollywood Heather, Nancy looked at Trina and Nadine. They both seemed pretty upset.

"Cake!" Mrs. Shannon sang as she walked in. Mr. Shannon followed. He was carrying a birthday cake glowing with candles. As he set it down everyone smiled. It was decorated with a picture of Hollywood Heather!

After everyone sang "Happy Birthday," Deirdre made a secret wish. Then she blew out the candles. "Let's eat, you guys!" she announced.

The cake tasted as good as it looked. Nancy was enjoying a big piece—until she dropped frosting on her cupcake pajamas!

"Oh, well," Nancy sighed. "Now I have choco-late frosting on my cupcakes."

Soon there was only one piece of cake left. Cassidy was about to reach for it when Deirdre said, "No, you don't. I'm the birthday girl, so I'm saving it for tomorrow."

"Meanie!" Cassidy said, stomping her foot.

After cake everyone painted each other's toe-nails purple, pink, and blue. A few minutes later, the girls began to yawn.

"We can't fall asleep!" Madison said.

"We're supposed to stay up all night!" Kendra said.

"I guess we have to remember that it's called a *sleepover*," Nancy said with a yawn, "and not a *wakeover*."

"I'm putting Hollywood Heather on the window-sill," Deirdre said, "so everyone can see her as we fall asleep."

She carried the doll to the windowsill. Since they were in the basement, the window was much higher than usual—too high for Deirdre to reach.

"Let me do it," Trina said. "I don't play basketball for nothing." She took Hollywood

Heather, reached up, and placed her carefully on the windowsill.

"Thanks," Deirdre said quietly.

"No problem," Trina answered.

The girls lined their gear up against the walls. Then Deirdre snapped a picture of everyone underneath the window.

"It's for my Web site," Deirdre said. "I want the whole world to know I have a Hollywood Heather doll!"

After brushing their teeth and

washing their faces, the girls unrolled their sleeping bags and snuggled inside. Nancy lay between Bess and George. When the lights were out, she could see Hollywood Heather shining in the moonlight.

"It's dark in here!" Cassidy suddenly whined. "No spooky stories, okay?"

"How about some jokes?" George asked in the dark. "Why can't you give a cookie to a teddy bear?"

"Why?" Cassidy's voice asked.

"Because they're always stuffed!" George said. Some girls laughed. Some groaned.

"My turn," Nancy said. "How do you know if an elephant's been in your refrigerator?"

"How?" Bess asked.

"Because," Nancy said. She could feel her eyelids getting heavier and heavier. "His footprints are in the . . . the . . . the . . ."

That was the last thing Nancy remembered before falling asleep. The next thing she knew, an arm was shaking her awake.

"Where is she?" Deirdre asked in a shaky voice. "Where's Hollywood Heather?"

"Huh?" Nancy asked. She rubbed the sleep out of her eyes. The room was light. The clock on the wall read eight o'clock.

Deirdre was walking between the sleeping bags.

"Where's Hollywood Heather, you guys?" she cried.

Nancy looked at the windowsill. Then she sat straight up. Hollywood Heather was gone!

CHAPTER FOUR

Cake to Case

"What happened to Hollywood Heather?" Nancy asked.

All the girls were wide awake now. They were sitting on their sleeping bags and staring at the window.

"That's funny," George said. "I went to the bathroom at six forty-five this morning. When I came back, the doll was on the windowsill."

"How do you know it was six forty-five?" Bess asked.

"I looked at the clock before I fell back to sleep," George explained.

"Did anyone see what happened to my doll?" Deirdre cried out.

All heads shook back and forth.

"Then help me find her!" Deirdre pleaded.

Nancy scrambled to stand up. She could see that one of the sleeping bags was empty. The basketball design on the bag told her it belonged to Trina.

"Hey, what happened?" a voice asked.

Nancy turned. She saw Trina walk into the room. Trina's eyes widened when Madison told her about the missing doll.

"Look everywhere," Deirdre instructed. "If you find Hollywood Heather, yell out at the top of your lungs!"

The girls searched the room for Hollywood Heather. They looked under tables, behind bookcases—even under sleeping bags. Nancy was about to look near the windows when she saw Cassidy. The little girl sat on top of her sleeping bag. She clutched a yellow and red backpack. The outside flap had a picture of the cartoon character Artie the Aardvark on it.

Why isn't she looking for the doll? Nancy wondered.

"Tell your mom and dad, Deirdre," Kendra said. "Maybe they can help us look."

"I can't!" Deirdre said. "I promised I'd take extra good care of Hollywood Heather."

"It's just a doll," Trina said.

"Just a doll?" Deirdre gasped. "Is the Statue of Liberty just a statue? Is the Great Wall of China just a wall? Is Johnny Appleseed just an apple?"

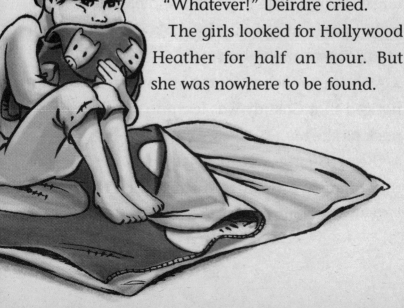

"He's not an apple," Andrea said slowly. "I think he planted apple trees or something."

"Whatever!" Deirdre cried.

The girls looked for Hollywood Heather for half an hour. But she was nowhere to be found.

"If anyone in this room took Hollywood Heather," Deirdre said, "tell me now."

The room was silent. Then Mrs. Shannon opened the basement door at the top of the stairs and called, "Girls! Breakfast is ready!"

They quietly climbed the stairs. Cassidy was still holding her Artie the Aardvark backpack.

Why is she bringing her backpack to breakfast? Nancy wondered.

Upstairs everyone sat down at the Shannons' dining-room table. Mr. and Mrs. Shannon served scrambled eggs and whole wheat toast. Nancy looked around the table as she ate. Deirdre was picking at her eggs with her fork. Her best friend Madison was pretty quiet too.

As Nancy reached for the strawberry jam, she noticed that Cassidy was leaning over her backpack as she ate.

"Bess, George," Nancy whispered. "Do you think maybe Cassidy took Hollywood Heather?"

"Why do you say that?" Bess asked.

"Cassidy won't let go of her backpack," Nancy said quietly. "And she is sort of a—"

"Pest," George finished.

After breakfast the girls went to the basement to collect their gear.

"Madison," Deirdre asked her best friend. "Can you stay and help me look for Hollywood Heather?"

"Can't!" Madison said quickly. "I have to go home and clean my room."

Deirdre frowned as Madison left the basement. When most of the other girls were gone, she looked sadder than ever.

"Don't worry, Deirdre," Nancy said. "Maybe the person who took Hollywood Heather will give her back soon."

"Sure!" Bess said cheerily. "Nancy even thinks she knows who took her."

"Bess!" Nancy hissed.

"Please tell me, Nancy!" Deirdre said, shaking Nancy's arm. "Who do you think took Hollywood Heather?"

"I don't know for sure," Nancy said. "So I don't want to say anything."

Deirdre looked disappointed. Suddenly her eyes lit up.

"I have a superific idea!" Deirdre said. "Why don't *you* find the person who took Hollywood Heather?"

"Me?" Nancy asked.

"You found the hidden goody bag," Deirdre said.

"And you're great at guessing things, Nancy," George said. "You always guess the school lunch."

"You even guessed Marshmallow's name!" Bess said.

"Yes," Nancy said. "But—"

"Come on, Nancy," George urged. "Don't you want to solve a real-life mystery?"

"You can be like—a detective!" Bess said.

A detective? I am pretty good at finding things and guessing things, Nancy thought. *I do like reading mystery books and watching mystery shows on TV with Daddy. So maybe solving a mystery would be fun . . . way fun.*

"I can try," Nancy said. "But I don't want to do it alone. Does anyone want to help?"

Bess's and George's hands flew up.

"I would if I could," Deirdre said. "But I have to practice my tap, gymnastics, and my recipe for Junior Chefs of America Club today."

"Do *you* think you know who took your doll, Deirdre?" Nancy asked.

Deirdre nodded. "Trina was the only one who could reach the window," she said. "And she came into the basement after the doll was missing. She was probably stuffing Hollywood Heather into her stinky gym bag!"

"But Trina is your friend," Nancy said. "Not your best friend like Madison—but still your friend."

"Maybe she wanted Hollywood Heather more than she wanted to be my friend," Deirdre sighed.

Nancy, Bess, and George stared at Deirdre as she left the basement.

"Wow," George said. "She's totally upset."

"I'm totally psyched," Bess said. "We're going to solve a real-life mystery, you guys!"

The three friends high-fived.

"Now that we're detectives," Nancy said, "where do we start?"

"Don't ask me!" George laughed. "I don't have a clue!"

"Clue!" Nancy exclaimed. "That's it! The first thing we do is look for clues!"

"Let's check the windowsill," Bess said. "That's the last place Hollywood Heather was before she disappeared."

They hurried to the window.

"It is high," George said. "How would a little kid like Cassidy reach the doll?"

Nancy pointed to a bench nearby. "She could have climbed up on that," she said.

The bench wasn't very heavy. The three girls moved it under the window. Then they all climbed up on it. Nancy checked the window to make sure it was locked. It was. Next she ran her hand along the windowsill. Instead of dust, there was some soft white fuzz all over it.

"Maybe it came from Hollywood Heather's

poncho," Bess said. "The wool was soft and fuzzy too."

"It was also green," George said. "This stuff is white."

"Then what is it?" Bess asked.

Nancy examined the wispy fuzz.

"I don't know," she said. "But I think we just found our first clue!"

CHAPTER FIVE

Clue Times Two

"Our first clue!" Bess exclaimed. "How cool is that?"

"Let's take some as evidence," Nancy said.

"Evi-dance? What's that?" Bess asked.

"That's a fancy word for proof," Nancy explained. "My dad explained it to me once when we were watching a mystery movie together."

Nancy tried to pick up the fuzz. But the wisps kept slipping from her fingers.

"Wait here," Bess said as she hopped off the bench. When she came back her hand was wrapped with sticky tape.

"What's that?" George asked.

"A clue mitt!" Bess said. "I built it myself."

Bess ran her sticky mitt over the window-sill. Clumps of fuzz stuck to the tape.

"Thanks, Bess!" Nancy exclaimed.

The girls jumped off the bench. Bess pulled the sticky mitt off her hand. She dropped it into an empty goody bag that she found on a table.

"Let's see what else we can find," Nancy said.

The girls moved the bench. They got down on their hands and knees and searched the cream-colored carpet.

Nancy saw something orange on the floor. She picked it up and rolled it around in her hand.

"It looks like a button," Nancy said. "It might be a clue."

"Two clues!" Bess squealed. "We're on a roll!"

"Now we have to figure out who would have taken Hollywood Heather," Nancy said as she dropped the button into the bag.

"You mean suspects?" George asked.

"How did you know?" Bess asked.

"Nancy isn't the only one who likes mysteries!" George said with a grin.

Nancy looked at the clock. It was almost time for Hannah to pick them up.

"Let's work on the case in my room," Nancy suggested. "We can keep our clues in my desk drawer. And we can use my computer to write down everything we find out."

"Did you say computer?" George said. She gave a thumbs-up sign. "I'm there!"

Bess and George called home for permission to go to Nancy's house. Then Hannah picked the girls up and drove them five blocks to the Drew home.

Nancy, Bess, and George all had the same rules. They had permission to walk up to five blocks as long as they were together. But with all their heavy sleepover gear, five blocks was too far to walk!

As soon as they reached the Drew house, the girls ran straight up to Nancy's room. Nancy carefully placed the clue bag in her top desk drawer. Then she turned on her computer.

George sat down at the keyboard. She opened up a new file and called it "Who Took Hollywood Heather?"

"What do we know so far?" Nancy asked.

"Hmm," George said. "The doll was on the windowsill at six forty-five this morning when I came back from the bathroom."

"Deirdre woke me up at eight," Nancy remembered. "So Hollywood Heather must have disappeared between about seven and eight o'clock in the morning."

"Type that in, George!" Bess said.

"I'm typing! I'm typing!" George said as her fingers flew across the keyboard.

"What about suspects?" Nancy asked.

"We have one already," Bess said. "Cassidy Rubin."

"Right," Nancy said. "Cassidy could have stuffed the doll in her backpack. Maybe that's why she wouldn't let go of it."

"Cassidy was also mad at Deirdre for not letting her have the last piece of birthday cake," George said. "Maybe she took Hollywood Heather to get even."

"That's it. Case closed!" Bess declared. "Cassidy took the doll!"

"We don't know for sure, Bess," Nancy said, shaking her head. "So far she's just a suspect."

George looked up the word "suspect" on the computer's spell-check. She typed it on the page, with Cassidy's name underneath.

"Who else could have taken Hollywood Heather?" Nancy asked.

Bess sat on Nancy's bed. She bounced a stuffed tiger on her lap. "Maybe Deirdre was right about Trina," she said. "Trina *was* mad at her. And she was the only one who could reach the windowsill."

"Anyone could have climbed up on something, though," George said. "Just like we did."

Nancy didn't want to blame Trina. But then she remembered something else. . . .

"Trina's sleeping bag was empty when the doll went missing," Nancy said. "Maybe she did go upstairs to hide the doll in her bag."

George added Trina's name to the suspect list.

"Do you think Trina's doll was a fake, like Deirdre said?" Bess asked.

"Let's check out the City Girls Web site," George said. "They have pictures of all the dolls. Maybe there's a picture of Indianapolis Ivy."

George saved their case file before going online. She was about to search for the City Girls site when she heard a little jingling noise.

"You've got an instant message, Nancy," George said.

Nancy leaned over to read her message. "It's from Pickles99," she said.

"Pickles? Who's that?" Bess asked.

"Brianne Slotsky from school," Nancy explained. "She puts pickles on all her sandwiches."

"Even peanut butter?" Bess gasped.

"Why wasn't Brianne at the sleepover?" George asked. "Doesn't she have a City Girls doll?"

"Not yet," Nancy said. "But that's all she ever thinks about!"

Nancy read the message out loud. "'Nadine called me. She said she has a new Hollywood Heather doll. Is it true?'"

All three girls stared at the message.

"You guys," Nancy said slowly. "Did she just say Nadine has Hollywood Heather?"

Chapter Six

Hide and Peek

"I forgot about Nadine!" George said. "She said Hollywood Heather should belong to her."

"Wasn't Nadine wearing orange pj's?" Bess asked.

"So?" George asked.

"The orange button clue!" Nancy exclaimed. "Good catch, Bess!"

Another message popped up from Pickles99. It said, "Hello? Are you there?"

"I forgot about Brianne!" Nancy said. She quickly typed, "It's news to me. Gotta go!"

"Now we have three suspects," Nancy said as she logged off. "Cassidy, Trina, and Nadine."

"Let's find them," George said. "And tell them we think they took Hollywood Heather!"

"No way, George!" Nancy said. "Good detectives always ask lots of questions before accusing anyone."

"What kind of questions?" Bess asked.

"That's what we have to figure out," Nancy said.

"Can we figure it out over pizza?" Bess asked. "I'm getting hungry."

"You just had scrambled eggs!" George said.

"That was three hours ago," Bess cried.

Nancy printed out their notes.

"A real case file!" she said. "How cool is that?"

Nancy got permission from her dad to go to Pizza Paradise on River Street. Hannah drove Bess and George to their houses to drop off their gear. Then Mrs. Fayne drove the girls to River Street in her van.

Mrs. Fayne owned a catering business. The back of the van was filled with containers of coleslaw and potato salad.

"I have to drop off this food at a bridal shower, girls," Mrs. Fayne said after she parked. "You go straight to the pizza parlor and I'll meet you there at two o'clock."

"Two o'clock?" Bess said. She glanced at her international watch. "Is that two o'clock in England, Italy, or China?"

"Show-off!" George said with a smirk.

Nancy glanced at her own watch. It said one fifteen. That gave them lots of time to eat pizza and talk about the case.

After saying good-bye to Mrs. Fayne, the girls walked up the block to Pizza Paradise. Halfway there Bess grabbed Nancy's arm and whispered, "Don't look now—but look who's there!"

"Bess!" Nancy said. "How can I not look and look at the same time?"

"Then—just look!" Bess whispered.

Nancy looked where Bess was pointing. Standing in front of a grocery store were Nadine Nardo and her mom.

"I don't want Nadine to see us yet," Nancy said quietly. "Let's hide somewhere."

River Street was lined with trees. Nancy, Bess,

and George ducked behind an oak tree with a thick trunk. They were close enough to hear Nadine and her mom talking.

"What you did was not okay, Nadine!" Mrs. Nardo was saying.

"But Mom!" Nadine said. "I had to have a Hollywood Heather doll. I just had to!"

The girls peeked out. Nancy saw Nadine holding a shopping bag at her side. She also saw two doll feet with white boots sticking out at the top.

"You guys," Nancy whispered. "Doesn't Hollywood Heather wear white boots?"

"You bet," George whispered. "If that isn't Hollywood Heather, I'll eat my socks!"

"Gross!" Bess cried.

"Shh!" Nancy said. "We have to see what's in the bag."

Mrs. Nardo went into the grocery store. Nadine stayed out by the gumball machines. She put the shopping bag on the sidewalk as she

48

searched in her waist pack for a quarter.

"Now's our chance," George whispered. "I'm peeking inside that bag!"

"That's snooping!" Nancy said doubtfully.

"We're detectives," George replied. "We're supposed to snoop."

While Nadine put her quarter into the gumball machine, George tiptoed toward her. She grabbed a handle on the shopping bag. But just as she was about to peek inside, a gumball rolled out of the machine onto the sidewalk. Nadine turned to catch it and saw George with her hand on the bag!

"George," Nadine said. "What are you doing?"

Oh, great, Nancy thought.

George froze with her hand on the shopping bag. "Um . . . looking for Hollywood Heather?" she said, looking up at Nadine.

"What?" Nadine cried.

Nancy and Bess ran over.

"First my gumball rolls away and now this!" Nadine stomped her foot. "Do you think *I* took Hollywood Heather?"

"Well," Nancy started to say.

"We know there's a doll in there, Nadine," George said. "Why don't you just let us look?"

Nadine grabbed a handle on the bag. "What are you, some kind of detectives?" she demanded.

"Bingo!" Bess replied with a smile. "How'd you guess?"

Nancy watched as George and Nadine played tug-of-war with the shopping bag.

"We just want to peek!" George insisted.

"You mean sneak!" Nadine said.

The girls kept tugging— until the bag tore in half and Hollywood Heather dropped to the ground! But when Nancy, Bess, and George looked at the doll, they gasped. Her skin was orange, her head

had short patches of white hair, and her brown eyes were smudged with colorful gunk!

"Omigosh, Nadine!" Nancy cried. "What have you done to Hollywood Heather?"

ChAPTER SEVEN

Party Artie

"Oh, don't have kittens!" Nadine said. She scooped up the doll. "It's not Hollywood Heather!"

"But didn't you tell Brianne Slotsky that you have a Hollywood Heather doll?" Nancy asked.

Nadine heaved a sigh. She touched her forehead with the back of her hand and said, "I wanted Hollywood Heather really badly. So I decided to turn New York Nikki into her."

Nancy, Bess, and George stared at the messy looking doll.

"You mean . . . that's New York Nikki?" George asked, pointing.

Nadine nodded sadly. "A dolly makeover— that was my plan," she said. "I gave her a tan by pouring on my mom's instant tanning lotion. It made her turn orange. I dyed her hair blond with my mom's hair dye. It made her hair break!"

"Wow!" Bess said. "Your mom uses a lot of stuff!"

Nancy cleared her throat. Mrs. Nardo was coming out of the store. "Is everything okay?" she called.

"Can we take New York Nikki to the doll hospital now, Mom?" Nadine asked. "So they can change her back to the way she was before?"

"Yes, Nadine," Mrs. Nardo sighed. "As long as you promise never to give your dolls makeovers again."

Nadine did look sorry for messing up her doll. "Promise," she said. She waved good-bye to Nancy, Bess, and George. Then she followed her mom up the street.

"How do we know that doll wasn't Hollywood Heather?" George asked. "I mean, Nadine could have messed *her* up!"

But as Nancy thought about the doll, something clicked. "That doll's eyes were brown," she said. "Aren't Hollywood Heather's eyes blue?"

"Bright blue!" Bess agreed.

"So that *was* New York Nikki," Nancy said. "Nadine didn't take Hollywood Heather after all."

"Good!" George said. "Now can we please get some pizza? My stomach is rumbling like a runaway roller coaster!"

The girls walked toward Pizza Paradise. Once inside, Nancy and Bess ordered cheese slices. George got pepperoni. They were about to bring their plates to a table when Nancy saw Madison Foley. She was carrying a plate too.

"Do you want to sit with us, Madison?" Nancy asked.

"Can't!" Madison said. "I'm taking my slice to a Pixie Scout meeting."

Then Madison hurried out of the restaurant.

"Madison is in the third grade like us," Bess said. "Don't only first and second graders go to Pixie Scouts?"

"Maybe she got left back for not selling enough cookies," George said with a shrug.

Nancy, Bess, and George sat down at a small round table. They ate their slices and drank water. Suddenly they heard someone yell, "I'm an alien from planet Pizza Pie!"

Nancy glanced up. It was Cassidy Rubin running around the pizza parlor. She was holding pepperonis over her eyes, just like she did at the sleepover.

"Are we lucky or what?" Bess asked. "Cassidy is one of our suspects."

Nancy could see Cassidy's backpack on another table.

"Look!" Nancy said. "There's the backpack she was holding at the sleepover."

"Maybe Hollywood Heather is still inside," Bess said.

"Forget it," George said, shaking her head. "I'm not peeking into any more bags."

"We don't have to peek," Nancy said. "I'll just *feel* the bag to see if there's a doll inside."

"Cassidy won't see you, anyway," Bess said. "She has pepperonis over her eyes."

Nancy stood up and walked quietly to the

other table. She reached over a paper cup for Cassidy's backpack.

"Oops!" Nancy gasped. She had knocked over the paper cup. Purple liquid was spreading across the table!

Nancy didn't want the backpack to get wet, so she quickly picked it up. That's when she heard Cassidy cry, "Help! Nancy Drew is stealing my backpack!"

"No, I'm not," Nancy reassured the younger girl.

Everyone in the pizza parlor was staring at

her, even Mr. and Mrs. Randazzo, the owners.

Cassidy ran over, dragging Marcy by the hand.

"You weren't stealing my sister's backpack, were you, Nancy?" Marcy asked.

"No," Nancy said. She handed the backpack to Cassidy. "I was just trying to find Hollywood Heather."

Marcy stared at Nancy. "My sister may be a pest," she said, "but she's not a thief!"

"Let's ask her," George said. She turned to Cassidy. "Where were you between seven and eight o'clock this morning?"

"That's a weird question to ask a little kid," Marcy said. "She can hardly tell time yet."

"Can so!" Cassidy said. "I was in the living room watching *Artie the Aardvark* on TV. Deirdre's mother said I could."

Nancy smiled. She used to watch *Artie the Aardvark* too, so she knew every cartoon by heart.

"What was the show about, Cassidy?" Nancy asked.

"It was funny!" Cassidy giggled. "Artie was learning how to ride a skateboard in the zoo!"

"What happened?" Nancy asked.

"What are you doing, Nancy?" Bess whispered.

"Who cares about Artie the Aardvark?" George asked.

Nancy kept on listening.

"Artie was riding the skateboard. It flipped over and he fell into the seal pond. Then the seal bounced Artie on his nose like a ball!" Cassidy laughed.

"That's right!" Nancy said.

"I think I get it," George said. "Cassidy knows everything about the show today. So she *was* upstairs watching TV!"

"Not downstairs stealing the doll," Bess added.

But Nancy wasn't totally sure yet.

"One more question, Cassidy," Nancy said. "Why wouldn't you let go of your backpack this morning?"

Cassidy clutched her backpack again. She stared at the floor as she shuffled her feet. "Because," she said, "I did take something!"

Nancy stared at Cassidy. Was it Hollywood Heather?

CHAPTER EIGHT

Recess . . . Confess

"What did you take, Cassidy?" Nancy asked. "Did you take the doll?"

"Yeah, Cassidy," Marcy said. "What's in the bag?"

Cassidy held out her Artie the Aardvark backpack. She lifted the front flap and said, "Stick your hand in and see for yourself."

Nancy reached into the backpack. She felt something mushy and sticky!

"Eww!" Nancy cried. She yanked out her hand. It was dripping with pink and white goo. "What is this stuff?"

"Whipped cream and strawberry filling," Cassidy explained. "After the *Artie the Aardvark* show I was hungry, so I went into the kitchen. I

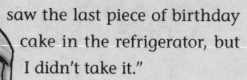

saw the last piece of birthday cake in the refrigerator, but I didn't take it."

"But!" George said. "It's all over Nancy's hand."

"I took it when Mrs. Shannon said I could," Cassidy said. "I didn't want Deirdre to know, so I put the piece in my backpack before everybody woke up."

Nancy held up her drippy hand.

So that's what Cassidy had in her backpack: the last piece of birthday cake!

"I can't eat it now," Cassidy said. "It's too mushy."

"That's for sure," Nancy muttered. She grabbed a stack of napkins to wipe her hand. Then she, Bess, and George left the pizza parlor.

"So far Nadine and Cassidy are innocent," George said. "That means we have only one suspect left."

"Trina Vanderhoof," Bess said.

It was two o'clock. As the girls waited for Mrs. Fayne in front of Pizza Paradise, Nancy was getting worried. What if Trina hadn't taken Hollywood Heather?

What if I never solve the case? Nancy wondered. *What will I tell Deirdre?*

"It's not easy being a detective, Daddy," Nancy said that night at dinner. "I have only one suspect left."

Mr. Drew wasn't a detective, but he was a lawyer. So he knew a thing or two about cases.

"Sometimes clues can lead to other clues, Pumpkin," Mr. Drew said as he buttered his roll.

"How?" Nancy asked.

Mr. Drew winked at Nancy and said, "I have a feeling you'll find out for yourself."

"I sure hope so, Daddy." Nancy sighed.

After dinner Nancy helped Hannah dry the

dishes. As she dried the last glass, the phone rang. Nancy put the towel on the counter and picked up the kitchen phone.

"Hello?" she said.

"Did you find my doll?" Deirdre's voice asked.

"Um . . . not yet, Deirdre," Nancy answered slowly.

"You have to find her by tomorrow afternoon!" Deirdre wailed. "My father is taking me to tea after school. He told me to bring Hollywood Heather!"

"You still didn't tell your parents that she's missing?" Nancy asked.

"I can't!" Deirdre said.

Nancy chewed her lower lip. It was already Sunday night. They would be in school the whole day on Monday. When would she work on the case?

"I still have to talk to Trina," Nancy said.

"Then go straight to Trina tomorrow and ask her where she hid my doll," Deirdre said. "Or look inside her basketball bag. Just be sure to hold your nose first!"

"I'll do the best I can, Deirdre," Nancy promised. She could hear Deirdre groan on the other end.

"First my doll disappears," Deirdre said. "Then my best friend Madison has no time for me. . . . My life is so hard!"

Nancy heard a click. Deirdre had hung up the phone. Nancy pressed the off button on the phone and turned around. Chocolate Chip was sitting behind her. The little brown puppy cocked her head as she looked up at Nancy.

"Wow, Chip," Nancy said. "Being a detective is a lot harder than I thought!"

"I still can't believe we have to solve the case by this afternoon!" George cried.

"That's just a few hours from now," Bess said. "How are we going to do that, Nancy?"

Nancy shook her head. It was Monday. The third and fourth graders were in the schoolyard for recess. Most of the kids were playing kickball. Some were on the swings. Others were shooting hoops on the basketball court.

"Deirdre wants me to question Trina today,"

Nancy said. "But I don't want to embarrass her in front of everybody."

"Me neither," Bess said.

"She also wants us to look inside her basketball bag," Nancy said.

"Nuh-uh!" George groaned. "That is one bag I'm definitely not looking into!"

"Did you bring our clues to school, Nancy?" Bess asked. "Maybe we can check them out some more."

Nancy pulled the plastic clue bag from her jacket pocket. Inside were the fuzzy tape and the orange button.

"My dad says that clues can lead to other clues," Nancy said. "But I still don't know what he means."

She dropped the bag back into her pocket. Just then a basketball rolled against her foot. Nancy looked up and saw Trina standing on the basketball court. Next to her stood Ned Nickerson from the fourth grade.

Nancy and Ned went to the same pediatrician. They used to play in the waiting room together when they were little.

"Throw it here, Nancy!" Trina called.

"Yeah, Nancy," Ned called. "Give it your best shot!"

"Okay," Nancy said with a smile. She picked up the ball. She was about to toss it when someone snatched it out of her hands.

"Hey!" Nancy said.

She turned and saw Deirdre clutching the ball. Her mouth was a grim line as she stared across the schoolyard at Trina.

"You're not getting it back, Trina Vanderhoof!" Deirdre shouted. "Not until you answer all of Nancy's questions!"

ChaPTER NiNE

Picture Perfect

"What do you want to ask me, Nancy?" Trina asked as she walked over. "Go ahead. Spill."

Nancy opened her mouth but nothing came out.

"How come you left the basement yesterday morning when my doll disappeared?" Deirdre blurted out.

"I had to," Trina said. "My nose was getting all tickly. Someone must have let Marshmallow in."

"I may have left the door open when I went to the bathroom," George said. "My bad."

"It's okay," Trina said. She raised an eyebrow at Deirdre. "Hey. You don't think I took Holly-wood Heather, do you?"

Deirdre stared back at Trina. She tossed the

basketball back at her and said, "Ask Nancy. She's the detective."

Nancy's jaw dropped as Deirdre ran away. She also saw Madison standing nearby. Madison was watching Deirdre as she ran away.

"Nancy?" Trina asked. "Do *you* think I stole Hollywood Heather?"

Nancy turned to Trina. She took a deep breath and said, "We thought you might have because you were out of the room. And you were the only one who could reach the windowsill."

"Oh," Trina said.

"And we found clues near the window," George said. "Show her, Nancy!"

Nancy took out the plastic clue bag. "We found an orange button and some fuzzy stuff on the windowsill."

"We're detectives now," Bess said. "In case you haven't noticed."

Trina stared through the clear bag. She frowned, stepped back, and said, "I know what that fuzzy stuff is!"

"What?" Nancy asked.

Trina opened her mouth to speak when—

"Hey, Trina!" Ned called. "We're waiting for the ball!"

"I'm there!" Trina answered. As she ran back to the court, she shouted over her shoulder, "And I didn't take Hollywood Heather!"

Then who did? Nancy wondered as she watched Trina jog toward the boys. Nancy noticed that Madison had disappeared.

"I believe Trina left because of Marshmallow," Bess said. "But why do you think she looked so weird when she saw the fuzzy stuff in the bag?"

"Yeah!" George chuckled. "You'd think she saw a cat!"

Cat. Nancy thought. *That's it!*

"Isn't Marshmallow a white cat?" Nancy asked.

Bess and George both nodded.

"And don't most cats like to sit on window-sills?" Nancy asked.

Her friends nodded again.

"Maybe Marshmallow came into the room, jumped from the gift table to the window-sill, and knocked down Hollywood Heather!" Nancy said.

"Okay," George said. "But wouldn't Hollywood Heather have fallen down somewhere?"

"We did look everywhere for the doll," Bess said. "So where did she fall?"

"That's the big question," Nancy sighed.

The school bell rang. Recess was over. Nancy, Bess, and George walked to the door with the other kids.

"Maybe there's still time to talk about the case after school," Bess said.

"Yeah," George agreed. "I already got permission to go to your house at three o'clock."

"Me too!" Bess said.

"Okay," Nancy said. "But time is running out."

They filed into Mrs. Ramirez's classroom. As Nancy sat at her desk, she tried not to look at Deirdre. She tried not to think about the case, but it kept popping into her head!

Where is Hollywood Heather? Nancy wondered. *Why can't I figure it out?*

After school the girls went to Nancy's house. After eating a snack of Hannah's yummy fruit salad, they went upstairs to Nancy's room. This time Nancy sat at the computer. Instead of opening the case file, she went online.

"There's got to be a site for junior detectives," Nancy said. "Maybe it has some tips on solving cases."

"Wait," George said. She pointed to the little red mailbox on the screen. "You got an e-mail."

Nancy clicked on the mailbox. Her e-mail was from KJack—Kendra Jackson. She wrote: "Check

70

out Deirdre's Web site. There are some neat pictures of all of us!"

Nancy found Dishing with Deirdre on the Web. There were lots of pictures from the sleepover. The girls smiled when they saw the group photo.

"Look!" Bess said. "There's Hollywood Heather on the windowsill before she disappeared."

Nancy gazed at the picture. There were lots of backpacks and duffel bags against the wall too.

"You guys," Nancy said. She leaned forward in her chair. "Could Hollywood Heather have fallen into a bag?"

"Maybe," Bess said. "But which one?"

George squeezed next to Nancy on the chair. She grabbed the mouse and clicked on the picture. Soon the picture was three times its original size!

Nancy studied the photo. She saw flashes of orange between everyone's feet. Maybe there was an orange bag under the window. Nancy pulled out the orange button and held it against the screen. They were the exact same color!

"I think this button came from the bag we

can see in the picture!" Nancy exclaimed. "But who had an orange bag at the sleepover?"

"Can't remember," Bess said, shaking her head.

"Let's check the other pictures," George said. She found shots of the guests walking to the house. One was of Madison carrying an orange duffel bag. It had orange buttons on the front flap!

"Madison's bag was under the window," Bess said.

Nancy couldn't take her eyes off the picture.

"Omigosh!" she gasped. "Does Deirdre's best friend have Hollywood Heather?"

ChaPTER TEN

Detectives Forever!

"But Madison is Deirdre's best friend, Nancy," Bess said. "If she found the doll, she would have told Deirdre."

"Unless Madison didn't want to tell her," Nancy said. "Let's go to Madison's house and ask her some questions. Anyone know where she lives?"

"She lives in that big blue house on Acorn Street," Bess said. "But I don't know how to get there from here."

"Piece of cake!" George said. With a few clicks of the mouse she found a site called Map Search. In a few seconds a map of River Heights was on the screen.

"Acorn Street is only four blocks away," Nancy said.

"We're allowed to walk there as long as we're together," Bess said, repeating their rules.

George printed out the map. "See?" she said. "There isn't anything you can't find on the computer!"

The girls asked Hannah's permission to go. Then they followed the map to the Foley house. Once there, Nancy rang the doorbell. Madison looked surprised when she opened the door.

"Hi," Madison said. "What's up?"

"Madison, did you find Hollywood Heather in your orange duffel bag?" Nancy asked.

Madison's eyes opened wide. She stepped outside and shut the front door behind her. "No way!" she said.

"Okay," Nancy said slowly. "Then did you lose a button?"

She pulled the orange button out of her pocket. Madison stared at it and said, "Maybe. So what?"

"We think Marshmallow the cat knocked Hollywood Heather off the windowsill," Nancy explained. "And since your bag was right under the window . . ."

". . . accidents happen," Bess finished.

Madison stared at the girls.

"It *was* an accident!" she finally said. "I found the doll in my bag when we were searching the room. I was going to tell Deirdre, but she seemed so mad. She would have thought I stole Hollywood Heather for sure!"

"But Deirdre's your best friend," George said.

"That's just it," Madison said. "I was afraid she wouldn't be my best friend anymore. And that would be awful!"

"So you let Deirdre think that Trina did it?" Bess asked.

When Madison heard Trina's name, she frowned. It made Nancy think of something else.

"Unless you were a little jealous of Trina," Nancy said gently. "For becoming Deirdre's second-best friend."

"I guess I was feeling a little sad about it," Madison said.

Nancy felt bad for Madison. It must have been superhard to keep such a big secret.

"But I still can't tell," Madison said, shaking her head. "Deirdre's dad is a big-shot lawyer. He could throw me into jail for stealing!"

"Nancy's dad is a lawyer too," Bess said with a smile. "He could get you out!"

"No one is going to jail, you guys!" Nancy said. "We can help explain everything to Deirdre."

"It's not that easy," Madison said. "There's another problem."

"What?" Nancy asked.

Madison ran into the house. She came back holding Hollywood Heather. Nancy looked at the doll. One of her arms was missing!

"How did that happen?" Nancy asked.

"It must have broken off when she fell into my bag," Madison said. She held up the broken arm. "How can I bring her to Deirdre like this?"

"Give her to me," Bess said.

Madison handed the doll to Bess. Everyone watched as Bess popped the arm right back in.

"How did you do that?" Madison gasped.
"Bess can build anything and fix anything," Nancy said cheerfully. "Now let's all go to Deirdre's house."

Deirdre lived around the corner from Madison. Mrs. Shannon greeted the girls and led them into the living room. Madison held Hollywood Heather behind her back as they waited for Deirdre.

When she came into the room, Deirdre was wearing a pink dress and black patent leather shoes.

"Hi," Deirdre said. "I'm going to tea soon—"

Madison pulled the doll out from behind her back. Deirdre took one look at it and her mouth dropped open.

"You found her!" Deirdre cried. She grabbed Hollywood Heather from Madison and held her tight. "Where was she?"

"I . . . I . . . I," Madison started to say.

"It's okay, Madison," Nancy whispered.

Madison took a deep breath. "Hollywood Heather fell into my bag," she blurted. "I didn't tell you because I thought you'd think I took her on purpose."

Deirdre stared at Madison. But then she smiled. "So *that's* why you've been too busy for me," Deirdre said. "Thanks for telling me the truth, Madison."

"So . . . you're not mad?" Madison asked.

"I'm just happy you're still my friend," Deirdre said. "Ever since Hollywood Heather went missing, you've been running away from me. I thought I did something wrong!"

"Sorry," Madison said. "But if it weren't for Nancy, I probably wouldn't have had the courage to say anything."

"I knew Nancy would find Hollywood Heather," Deirdre said.

"You mean Nancy, Bess, and George!" Nancy said.

Deirdre hugged Hollywood Heather. "Now I can take Hollywood Heather to tea with me," she said. "Just like my dad said I should."

Then she looked up and said, "Why don't you *all* come to tea? There'll be sandwiches and little cakes and minty tea—"

"I love little cakes!" George said.

"And big cakes!" Bess said, licking her lips.

It sounded good to Nancy, too. But she wanted Deirdre and Madison to fix up their friendship together.

"Thanks, Deirdre," Nancy said. "But we have to go home."

"I know!" Madison said. She turned to Deirdre and smiled. "Let's ask Trina to come with us. She's our second-best friend."

"Okay!" Deirdre said. "And guess what?"

"What?" everyone asked at the same time.

"There *is* a City Girls doll called Indianapolis Ivy," Deirdre said. "So I was wrong and Trina was right!"

Deirdre and Madison walked Nancy, Bess, and George to the door. As the three friends left the house, Madison called after them, "You guys should solve more mysteries. You're great at it!"

Walking down Acorn Street, Nancy thought about what Madison said. Maybe she was right. . . .

"You guys," Nancy said. "Maybe we *should* solve more mysteries!"

Bess and George stopped walking.

"You mean like a team?" George asked.

"Like a *club*!" Nancy said excitedly. "We can meet in my room to talk about our cases. And we can put all of our clues in my desk drawer just like we did for this case!"

"And I can write everything on your computer!" George said, her dark eyes flashing. "That was awesome!"

Bess gave a little excited hop. "And I can fix whatever breaks," she said. "And build some neat spy gadgets, too."

Nancy smiled. Their new detective club was

sounding better and better. But one thing was missing. Something very important . . .

"We need a name," Nancy said. "How about . . . the Mystery Girls?"

"Too old-fashioned," George admitted. "How about . . . Case Crackers?"

"We'd sound like a crunchy snack!" Nancy giggled.

"Let's see," Bess said. She twirled a lock of her hair as she thought. "What about . . . the Clue Gang?"

"Hmm," Nancy said. "Something that rhymes might be nice."

"Like what?" George asked.

"Like the Clue . . . the Clue . . ." Nancy started to say. Her eyes lit up. "The Clue Crew!"

The girls high-fived.

"Our own detective club!" Bess cried. "How cool is that?"

"Supercool!" Nancy agreed. "But do you want to know the best part?"

"We're going to be solving all kinds of cool cases?" George asked.

"No," Nancy said.

"What?" Bess asked.

"We're going to be solving all kinds of cool cases . . . *together*!" Nancy said with a smile.

Nancy Drew and the Clue Crew could hardly wait!

Head-To-Toe PJ Fashion Show!

Go glam at your next sleepover with a pajama fashion show! But before you strut down the runway in your favorite pj's, top off the look—and the fun—with hats made by you and your friends!

Get started with these cool chapeaus . . .

1. Hearts and Flowers Crown:

You will need:
1 paper plate
Construction paper
Paint, markers, or crayons
Scissors
Glue

Cut a slit down the middle of the paper plate. Leave about an inch around the edges of the plate. Cut three more slits the same size. These slits should cross the first one. Bend the points out to look like a crown. Using glue—and your imagination—attach paper hearts and flowers to points and sprinkle with glitter all around. You glow, girl!

2. Paper Bag Hat
You will need:
- 1 large paper grocery bag
- Scissors
- Stapler
- Markers or crayons
- Glue
- Feathers, ribbon, buttons, glitter, etc.

Draw a hat shape on the grocery bag. Cut out two of the shapes. Staple two pieces together. Using glue, go wild with feathers, ribbons, glitter—whatever you want to decorate! From supermarket to supermodel—your grocery bag hat will rule the runway!

Now you're ready to wear it . . . and work it!

HUNGRY FOR MORE MAD SCIENCE?

CATCH UP WITH FRANNY AS SHE CONDUCTS OTHER EXPERIMENTS!

Jump into history!
Read all the books in the

series!

#1 Lincoln's Legacy

#2 Disney's Dream

#3 Bell's Breakthrough

#4 King's Courage

#5 Sacagawea's Strength

Coming Soon:

#6 Franklin's Fame